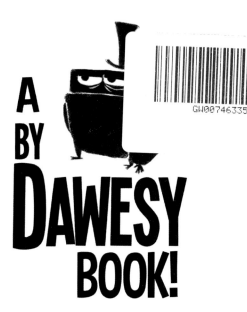

A
BY
DAWESY
BOOK!

Adventures of the...
WONDER FLEA
(THE WONDERFULLY WONDERFUL WONDER FLEA)

WRITTEN & CREATED BY

OLIVER DAWES

ILLUSTRATED BY JAMES WILLETTS

ISBN 978-1-5272-2165-9

First published in the UK 2018

www.bydawesy.com
www.james-willetts.co.uk

Printed and bound in the UK

It's me; it's me, the Wonder Flea!

Sent to protect our community,

Don't listen to people; I'm not what you think,

I don't suck blood, I think it stinks!

It makes me gag, sick as a pig,

It's not very clever and

not very big.

So instead,

I save the day,

From other suckers

that see you as prey.

I'm not a parasite, the opposite in fact,

I wear a cape and keep you intact.

My world is small, so teeny tiny!

It's hard to see me, especially my heinie!

But what's that I hear? I must dash,

From zero to hero, I've critters to bash!

I once felt confused, like I didn't belong,

My purpose in life, something was wrong.

I'm not like the others; I do my own thing,

And now I understand, I'm so happy I could sing!

Shout from the rooftops, whistle like the birds,

Listen to me! And these magic words:

Look up high, high in the sky,

My enemy flies, floats and quotes...

"I am so thirsty;

it's time to drink,

no time to question,

wonder or think!

I am the Mozzie! it's what I do;

move out the way, now let me through."

Stop what you're doing,

stop right now!

I won't let this happen;

you'll make them shout OWWWWW!

Show them some kindness,

why not instead?

Give them some flowers,

or a cuddly ted?

Oh my days, who stands before me?
It's the wonderfully wonderful Wonder Flea!
Not again!! You always stop me,
Can't you leave me, let me be free?

But I've got to drink; it's what I am,
I can't help it, I wasn't born a man.
With a choice of foods, from cherries to ham,
I suck blood! I am what I am!

Not a chance,

not on my nelly,

What you do is mean

and smelly.

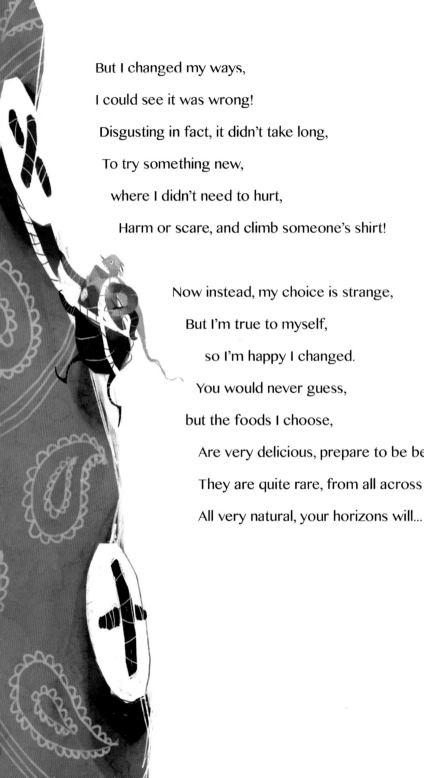

But I changed my ways,

I could see it was wrong!

Disgusting in fact, it didn't take long,

To try something new,

where I didn't need to hurt,

Harm or scare, and climb someone's shirt!

Now instead, my choice is strange,

But I'm true to myself,

so I'm happy I changed.

You would never guess,

but the foods I choose,

Are very delicious, prepare to be bemused.

They are quite rare, from all across our land,

All very natural, your horizons will...

DURIAN

Native to South East Asia

Spikey and pungent with a

savoury smell.

DRAGON FRUIT

Native to Mexico

Dramatic appearance with

a subtle flavour.

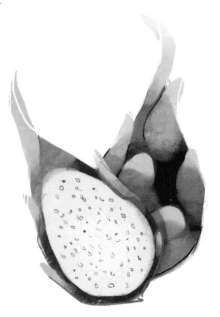

PASSION FRUIT

Native to South America

Juicy seeds you can scoop with a

spoon.

KIWANO

Native to Sub- Saharan Africa

Spikey skin, yellow and

green seeds.

Well I never!

That does sound fun,

To find something different,

my outlook has begun.

But it's not just me you need to convince,

There's someone else, follow these prints…

They're not so easy, not so nice,

Stubborn in fact, look, it's the lice!

YUMMY YUMMY

get in my tummy,

Fill my belly with

something scrummy.

I'll climb that hair,

which I call the ladder,

The ladder to blood,

that will fill my bladder!

No, No, No!

Stop, Stop, Stop!

I'll pull you down

with a hip and a hop.

I am he, it is but me,

The wonderfully wonderful Wonder Flea!

If you come down, you'll soon see,

The knowledge I'll give, will hand you the key!

Who are you?

What do you want?

Can't you see I'm busy

climbing this bouffant.

Oh I've heard of you!

The whispers are true,

spreading your point of view.

Well it better be special,

to tempt me down,

And turn this frown

upside down.

I'm telling

you now,

I'm very headstrong,

My meal times are important,

should you be wrong!

You're

in for a treat,

a mental ride,

Intellect that can't be pied!

Listen to me,

get down from that ladder!

I've something to share...

...AND FOOD TO GATHER!

ROMANESCO

Native to Italy

Looks like an alien, or exotic

cauliflower

FIDDLEHEADS

Native to North America

Green curly wurly

veggies

OCA

Native to South America

Tangier and sweeter than a...

potato

NOPALES

Native to America

Looks like a

cactus

I'm shocked I'm surprised,

what have you done?

I'm climbing down from this hair bun.

Stop your talking,

I'm too excited,

To source some nourishment,

My hunger ignited!

A world of flavour, for me to enjoy,

I'm now running off there's food to destroy!

Enlightenment you feel,

I'm so pleased to see!

A whole world of food,

for you and me!

Well the lice may be rude but at least they listen,

And now their new appetite discovered

and glistened!

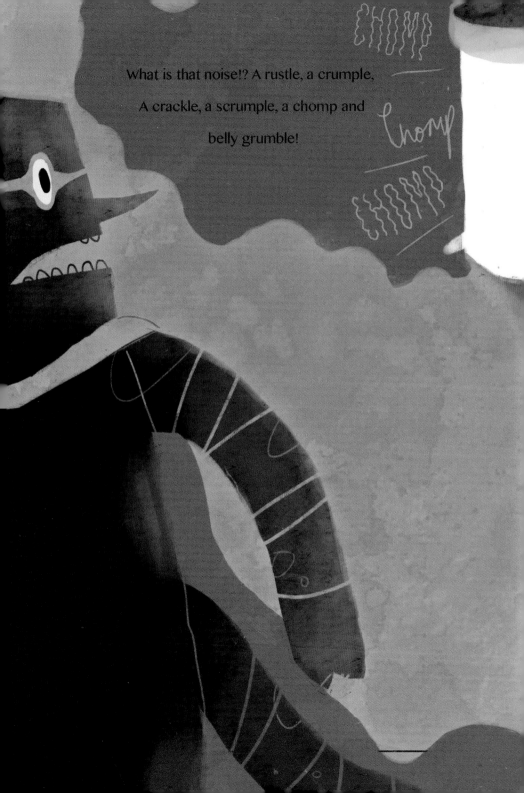

What is that noise!? A rustle, a crumple,

A crackle, a scrumple, a chomp and

belly grumble!

CHOMP

Chomp

CHOMP

Well at least they listencd; they gave it a bash,

Although I wouldn't have recommended going through the trash,

That must be smelly and pretty grim,

But it's better than biting her or him.

So I saved the day, I saved some skin,

From the Mozzie and lice biting your shin.

I am the hero, and your good friend,

I'll serve and protect

until the end.